DC SUPER-PETS!™

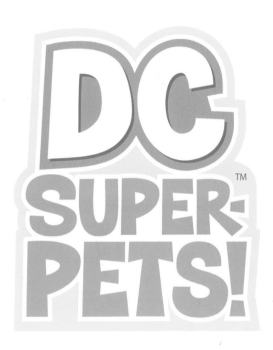

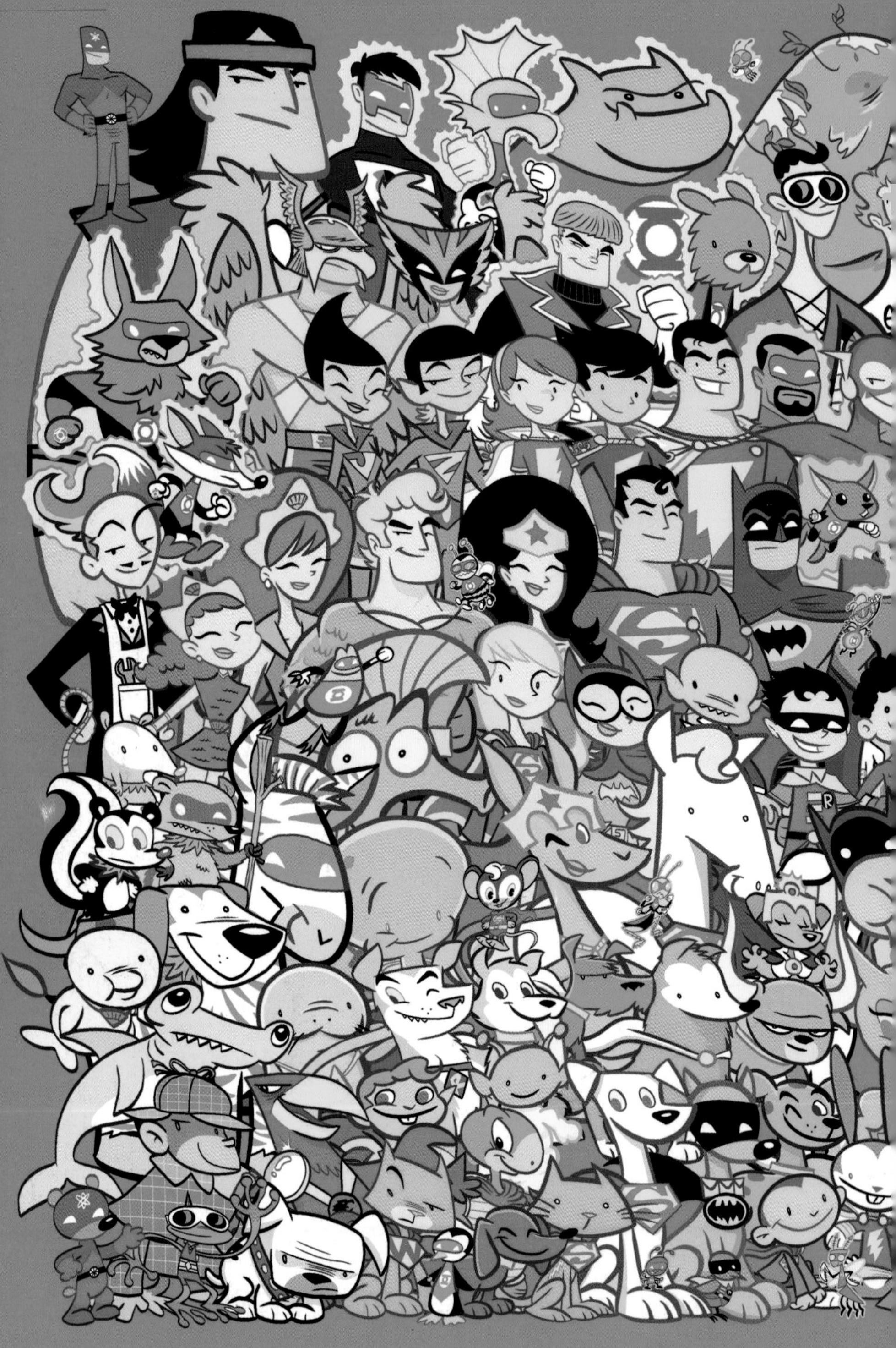

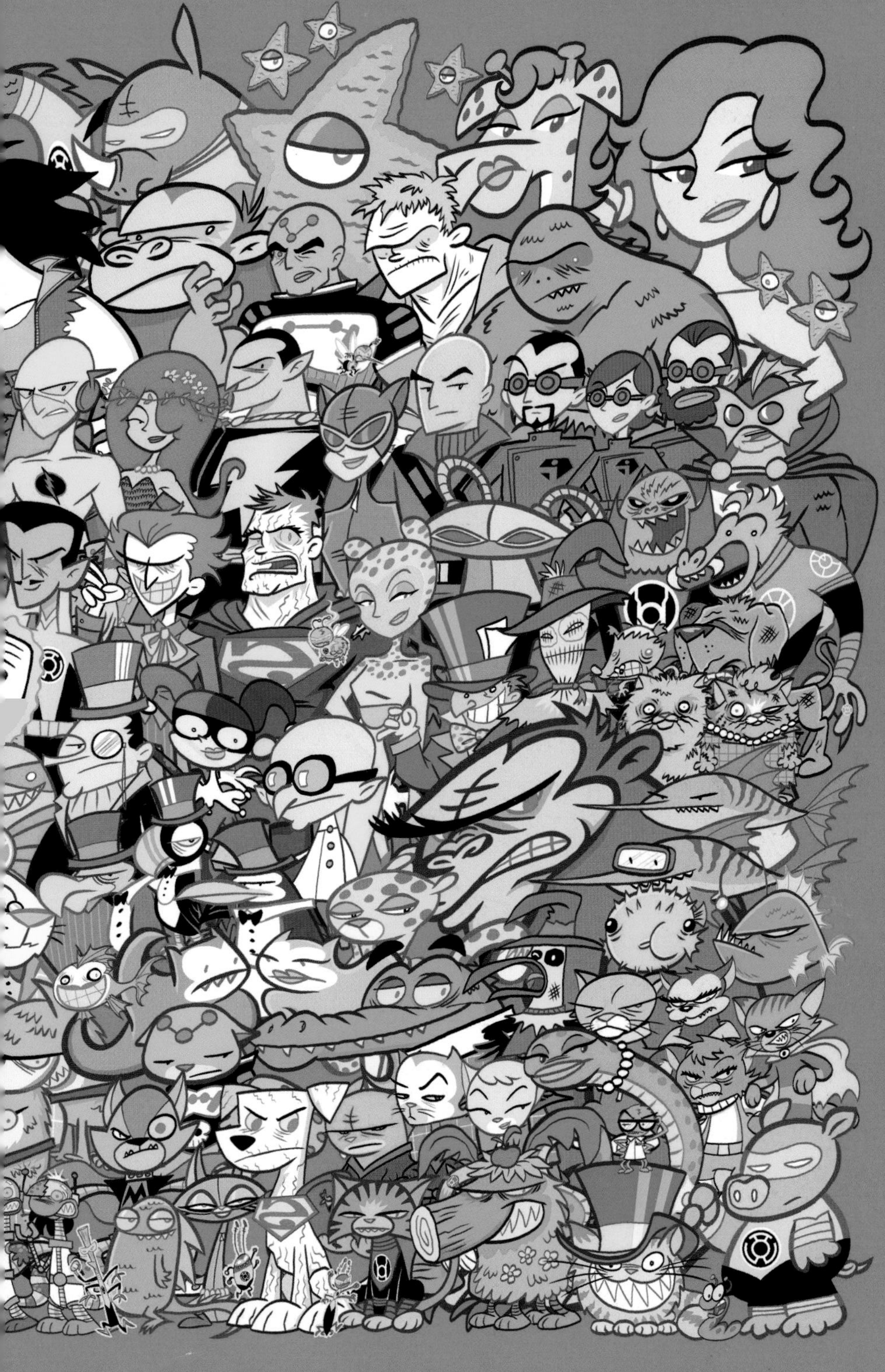

DC SUPER-PETS!

by John
Sazaklis

THE BIGGEST LITTLE HERO

illustrated by
Art Baltazar

The Atom / Ray Palmer
created by Gardner Fox

Picture Window Books™
a capstone imprint

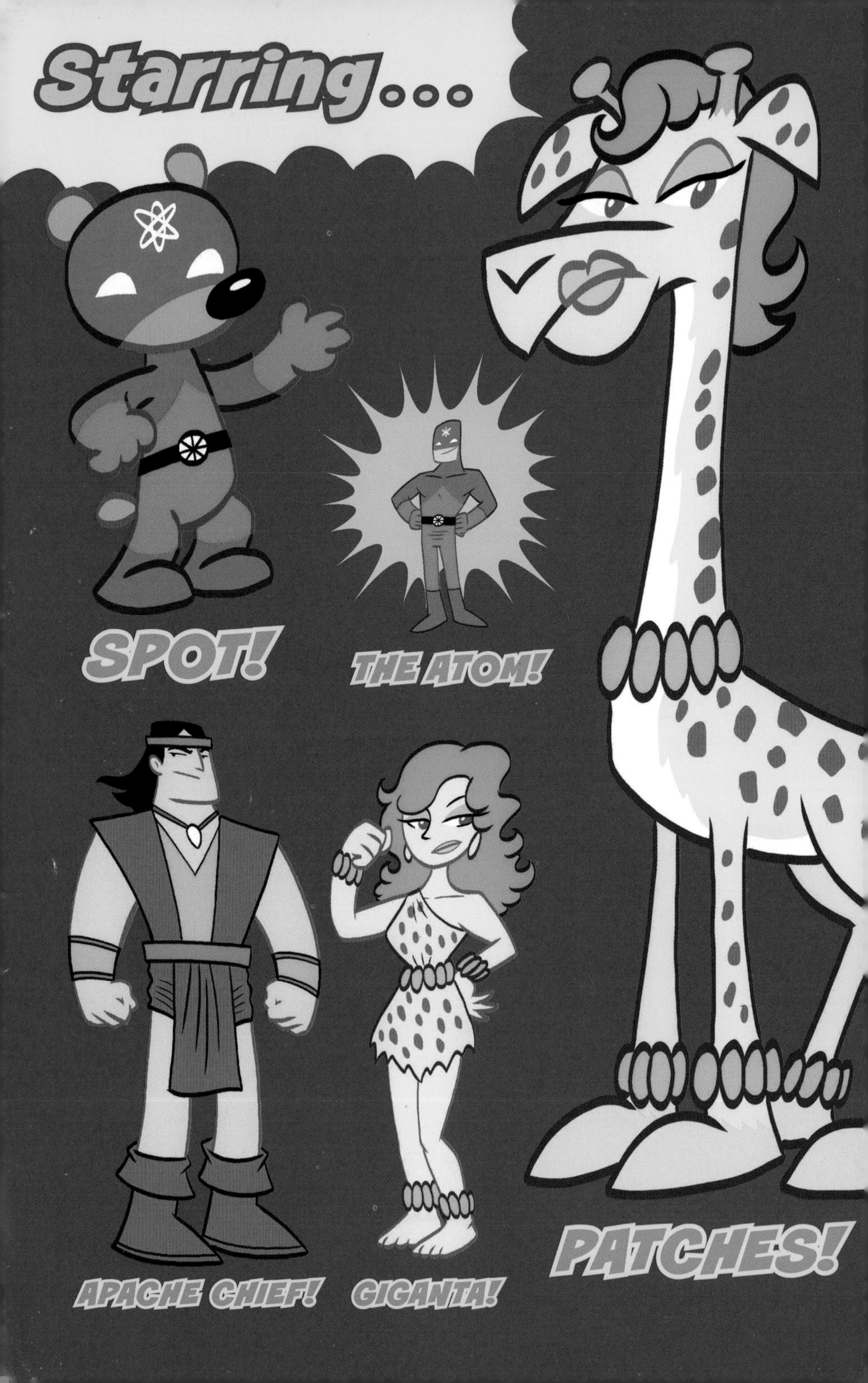
Starring...
SPOT!
THE ATOM!
PATCHES!
APACHE CHIEF!
GIGANTA!

TABLE OF CONTENTS!

Ivy Town University DATABASE

SUPER-PET HERO FILE 020:
SPOT

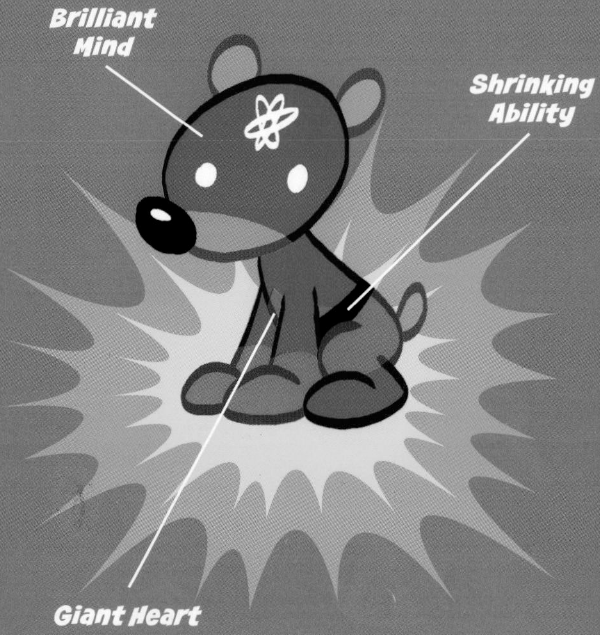
Brilliant Mind
Shrinking Ability
Giant Heart

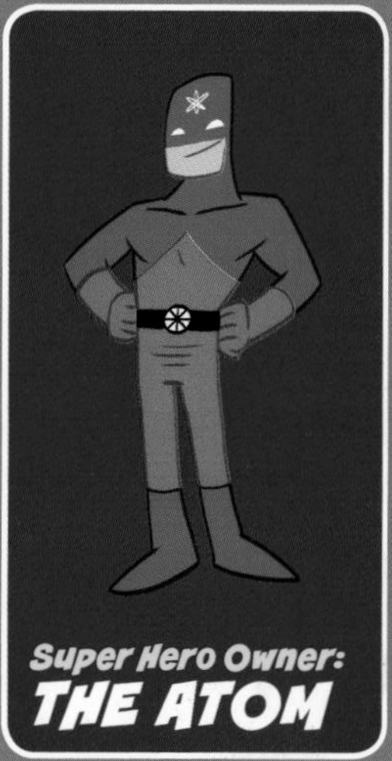
Super Hero Owner:
THE ATOM

Species: Canine

Place of Birth: Earth

Age: Unknown

Favorite Food: Baby Carrots

Bio: Aided by his master's invention, this common canine became a mighty mite, able to shrink and travel through phone lines.

Super-Pet Enemy File 020:
PATCHES

Roughneck

Giant
Size

Super-villain Owner:
GIGANTA

Chapter 1

MIGHTY MITES

One bright morning, **Dr. Ray Palmer** was preparing breakfast. **RUFF! RUFF!** His loyal dog, **Spot**, brought him the newspaper from outside.

Dr. Palmer dropped everything. He read the headline: **WHITE DWARF STAR FALLS TO EARTH!**

Ray was a professor at **Ivy Town University.** He taught the science of making things smaller. Spot was Ray's assistant, best friend, and an incredible canine scientist. Together, they were working on a new shrinking machine.

"This is it, Spot!" Ray cried. "You've solved the puzzle! We must get to the crash site before it's too late!"

Ray and Spot scarfed down some bacon and eggs. Then they dashed out of the house.

WHOOSH!

The newspaper said that the white dwarf star had exploded overnight. The pieces had rained down on the Ivy University football field. When Ray and Spot arrived, the field was blocked off with yellow tape.

The professor showed his I.D. badge, and the police let him in. Together, he and Spot scooped up as much of the star dust as they could.

"This dust is the key to our success," Ray told Spot. **"To the lab!"**

The tireless twosome worked late into the night. With Spot's help, Ray created a lens using the dust from the white dwarf star. When light passed through the lens, it could shrink any object. They tested the device on a nearby chair.

ZZZZWWWIP!!

The chair disappeared! It was no longer visible to the naked eye. Ray leaned over the empty space with a magnifying glass. Sure enough, there was the chair, as tiny as can be!

"We've done it, Spot!" cheered the

professor. Then Ray laid his head down

on the desk. He started snoring.

Spot curled up next to his master.

The pooped pooch fell asleep too.

The next day, Ray woke up on the floor of his lab. "Wake up, Spot," he said. "We still have work to do!"

Ray had another brilliant idea. He decided to reverse the shrinking device. He aimed the lens at the tiny chair and zapped it back to normal size.

 "Let's try it on ourselves," Ray said.

 "Bark!" Spot agreed.

The professor created uniforms that could shrink safely. At the same time, the suits would make them stronger.

Each suit contained a lens with the dwarf star dust. The lens was located on the belt. Pushing a button turned on the device.

 **"Ready, Spot?"** Ray asked his brave bowwow. **"Let's go!"**

 Ray and Spot both pressed the buttons on their belts.

SHWOOOOM!

Suddenly, the duo shrank to the size of atoms, the teeniest, tiniest elements on Earth.

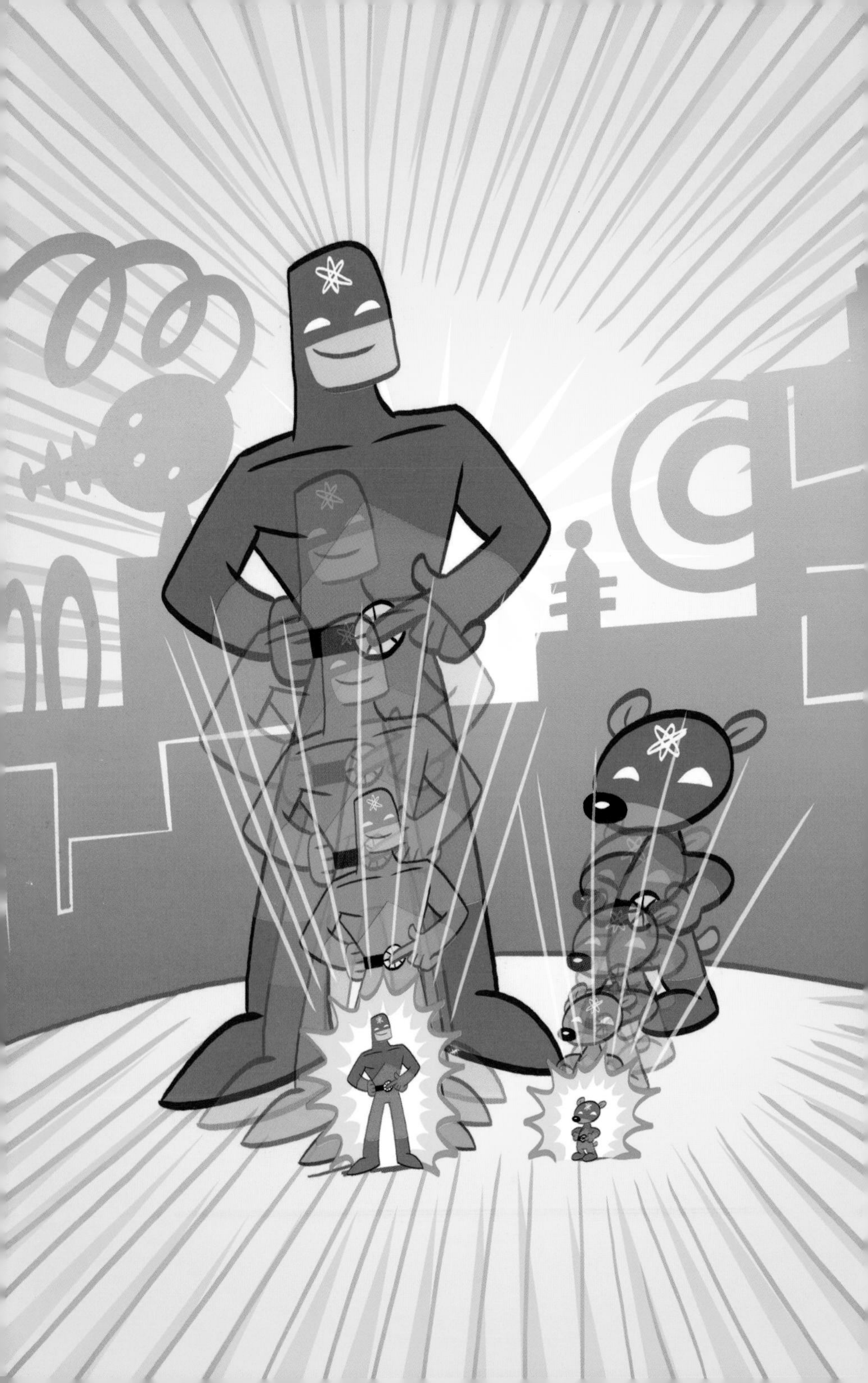

SHWOOOOM! In an instant, they were back to normal size again.

"This is amazing," Ray said. "I must tell Dr. Zeul!"

Ray picked up the telephone. He called **Doris Zeul.** She worked in the lab next door. She was developing a top-secret project too. It was the complete opposite of Dr. Palmer's.

Doris wanted to *increase* an object's size, giving anything the power of a giant! She needed only one more ingredient to complete her projects.

When the phone rang at her lab, Doris picked it up. "Hello?" she asked. But there was no answer. "Is anyone there?" she asked again.

"We're right here!" said a voice near her ear.

"Ah!" Doris screamed. She spotted Ray and Spot crawling out of her phone receiver.

 **"How did you do that?!"** she cried out.

Ray explained what happened. "We can shrink to the size of an atom," he said. "Then we can travel through phone lines by hopping on top of moving electrons. That's how we got here. Isn't that grand?"

Dr. Zeul was amazed and happy. She was also very jealous.

BEEP! BEEP! BEEP!

Suddenly, an alarm rang out. Several science students were trapped in a nearby elevator. They were carrying boxes of chemicals.

The elevator was out of control and kept jerking up and down. The chemicals were highly dangerous. They could explode at any moment!

Ray and Spot ran to the main lobby and used the emergency phone. They traveled through the phone line and into the elevator. **WHOOSH!**

Ray appeared on the shoulder of a student. "Hello there," he said.

"Ah!" the kid cried, dropping a box of beakers.

Ray changed to his normal size. He caught the box before it crashed.

WOOF! WOOF! Spot told the students not to panic.

He and his owner shrank again. They squeezed through the elevator's ceiling. Then they climbed into the machine's powerful gears.

Ray and Spot used all of their might.
They held the elevator in place until
everyone could get off safely.

Afterward, students and teachers
greeted them in the lobby. "Thanks so
much!" they told the heroes.

"Who are you?" asked a student.

Ray rubbed his chin. He thought of a good super hero name. "I'm **the Atom!**" Ray exclaimed. "And this is my partner — uh . . . **Spot!**"

"**Ruff!**" Spot yipped with excitement.

Chapter 2

GIANT PROBLEM

Dr. Zeul was a rainbow of emotions. She was red with anger, green with envy, and blue with sadness.

"My research is so much better!" Dr. Zeul whined. "I should have made that discovery. I should be getting all the attention!"

To feel better, Dr. Zeul headed to the traveling Super Hero Show. Performers at the show displayed their superpowers for loyal fans.

The star of the show was Apache Chief. This super hero could use a special magic powder to increase his size and strength. When Apache Chief spoke the magic word — "Inuk-chuk!" — he grew fifty feet tall!

Apache Chief called several animals on stage. The powerful hero picked up a giraffe. He held her in the air.

The crowd went wild.

Dr. Zeul's eyes widened with awe.
"Ray Palmer had his lucky break,"
she said, eyeing Apache Chief's magic
powder. "Now I've found mine!"

After the performance, Doris snuck into Apache Chief's dressing room. She snatched his magic powder and scooped out a handful.

Before she could use it, **Patches** the giraffe stuck her head into the room. The hungry animal licked it all up!

"Hey!" Doris cried. "Keep your neck out of my business!" Then she poured the rest of the powder on herself.

"Inuk-chuk!" she yelled.

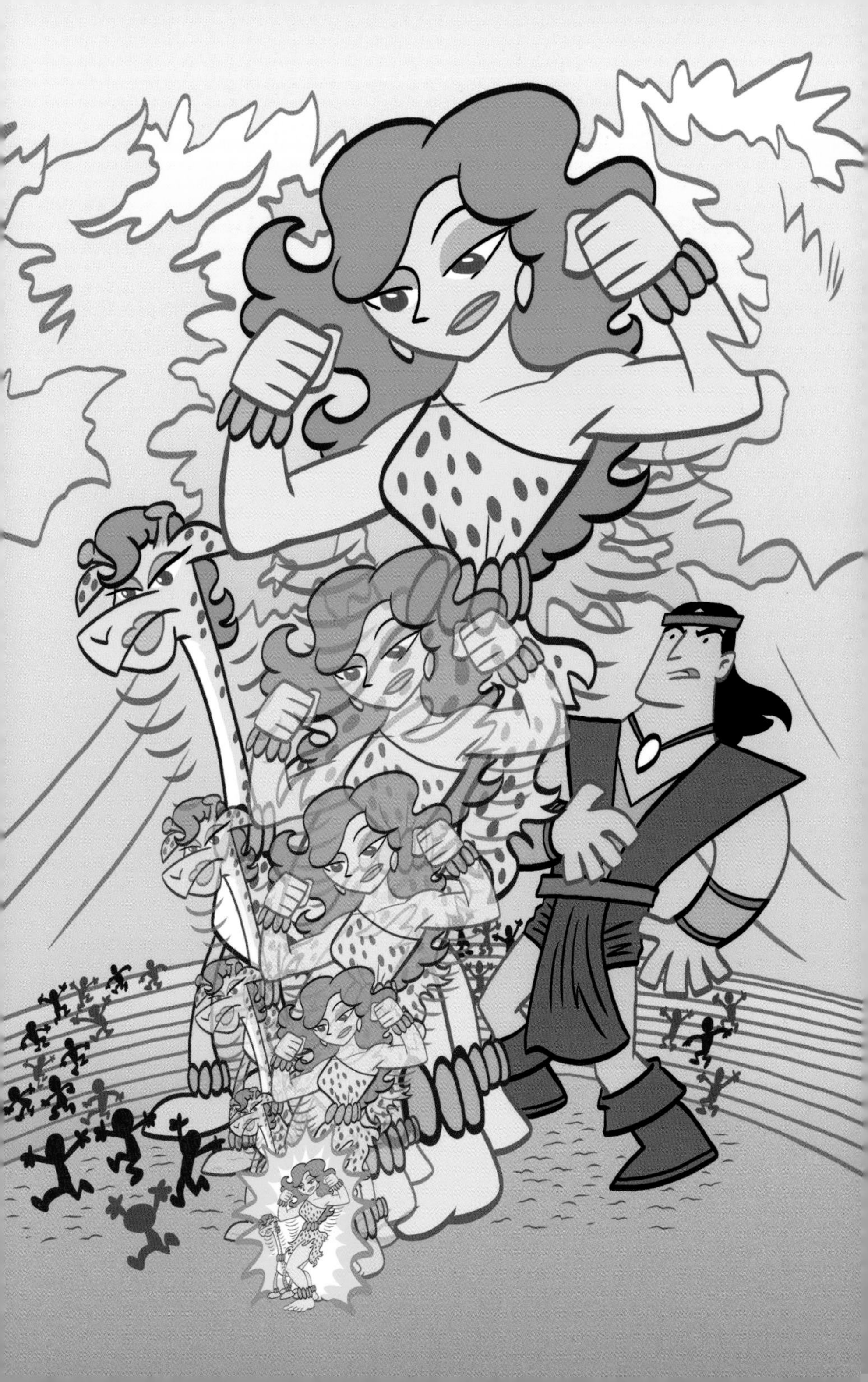

Doris and Patches stretched and ripped through the performance tent. They grew in size until they towered over the town. People ran screaming in all directions.

"I am Giganta!" cried the new villain. **"All of Ivy Town will look up to me!"** She turned and stomped away. Patches galloped after her.

Apache Chief discovered that his magic powder had been stolen. He felt as if he was to blame for the town's newest terror.

Apache Chief called Dr. Ray Palmer. Little did he know that his old friend was now a new hero — the Atom!

The Atom and Spot traveled through the phone lines and soon arrived at the circus. Apache Chief told them what had happened. Together, the three heroes set off to find Giganta and Patches. They were pretty sure the pair wouldn't be hard to miss.

Giganta and Patches thundered through the diamond district. The large looters went on a crime spree.

The villainess grabbed a hot air balloon out of the sky. She turned it upside down, making a loot bag. Patches stretched her long neck down the block.

CHOMP! CHOMP! The giraffe chewed the roofs off of jewelry stores.

Giganta followed close behind. She collected entire jewelry counters and dropped them into her new super-sized satchel. The giantess had thought of a plan. She would continue her research with the use of these jewels.

By crushing them into a fine dust, she'd combine them with Apache Chief's magic powder and multiply her powers. Giant size and super-strength were only the beginning. Today, Ivy Town. Tomorrow . . . the world!

Giganta spotted a large billboard, which read: **GLASSES BY GAUDET.** There was a large pair of oversized sunglasses on the sign. Giganta ripped them off. She put the glasses on.

"Don't I look divine?" she asked.

The store owner came running out. "What's the big idea?!" he yelled.

"I am!" shouted Giganta. She threw off the giant glasses and stomped away. The town was in trouble, and there was no one around to save it!

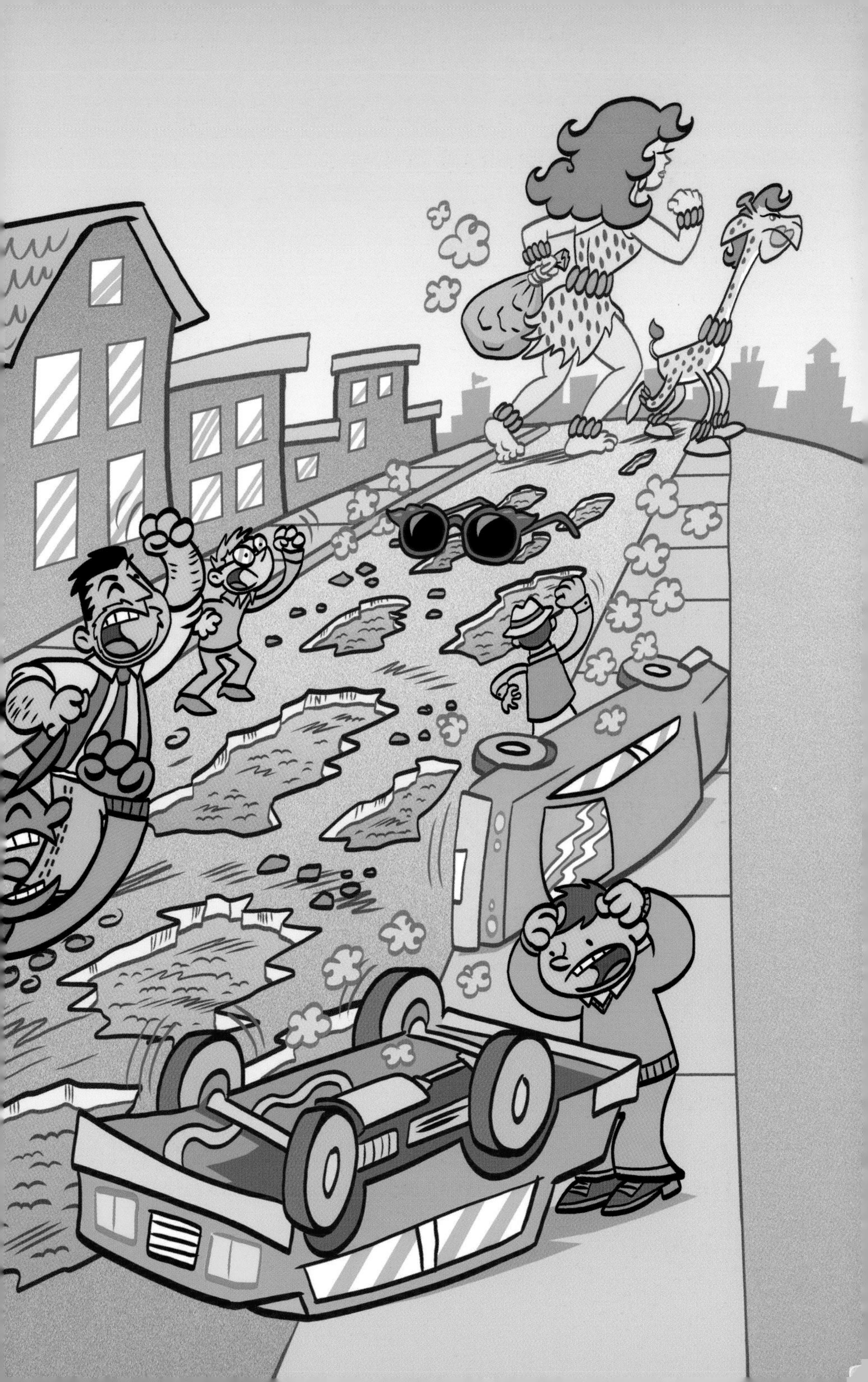

BIG FINISH

Finally, the three heroes arrived at the town square. They saw crushed police cars. They spotted giant footprints left in Giganta's path.

"This is all my fault," Apache Chief said. "There must be a way to stop her. I can grow in size and take her down!"

"Don't blame yourself," said the Atom. "Doris has gone mad with power. I'll try to reason with her first."

SHWOOOOM! The Atom and Spot zoomed through a nearby power line. They appeared on Giganta's shoulder.

 **"Doris, it's me,"** Ray said. "Please stop! We can talk about this."

Giganta grabbed the hero. **"I'll crush you like a bug!"** she shouted.

Spot hopped off Giganta's shoulder and landed on Patches' neck. Then he ran all the way up to the giant giraffe's head. Spot bit Patches on the ear.

CHOMMMP! Patches bucked her head back and forth trying to shake Spot off. The petite pooch bit Patches again and held on for dear life.

Giganta squeezed the Atom harder.

The hero couldn't reach his belt. He

was stuck. Spot thought up a better

idea. He leaped down into Patches' ear.

Spot cleared his throat and let loose a

loud bark.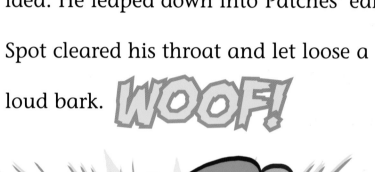

The sound echoed through the giant giraffe's ear canal. Patches got confused and fell forward, knocking into Giganta. Her grip on the Atom loosened, and the mighty mites rode an air current to safety.

The towering terrors tumbled down into a nearby park. Their huge bodies sank into the ground. Scared citizens ran away, afraid of being crushed.

The Atom had another plan. He and Spot were going to use their shrinking devices on Giganta and Patches.

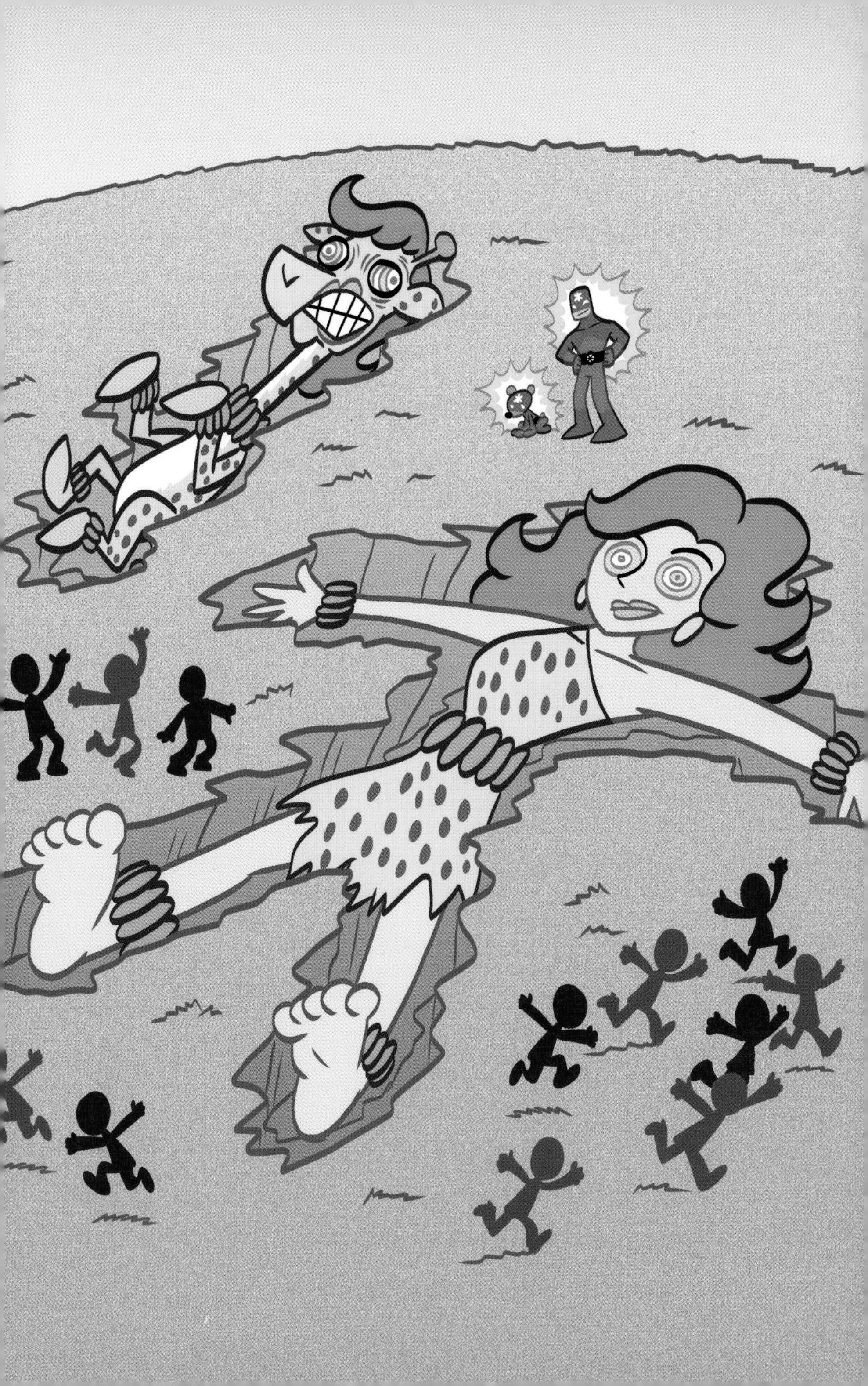

Once the lenses on their belts had
been reversed, the hero and his pet
raced over to the villains. They aimed
at them with the shrinking rays.

 "Stop that, you little gnat!"

Giganta yelled.

She and Patches tried to catch the
Atom and Spot. Giganta clawed at
the ground with her nails. Patches
stomped with her hooves.

But the half-pint hero and mini-mutt were too quick. Atom and Spot continued to hop around. They zapped the villains with their shrink-rays.

Until . . .

SHWOOOOM!

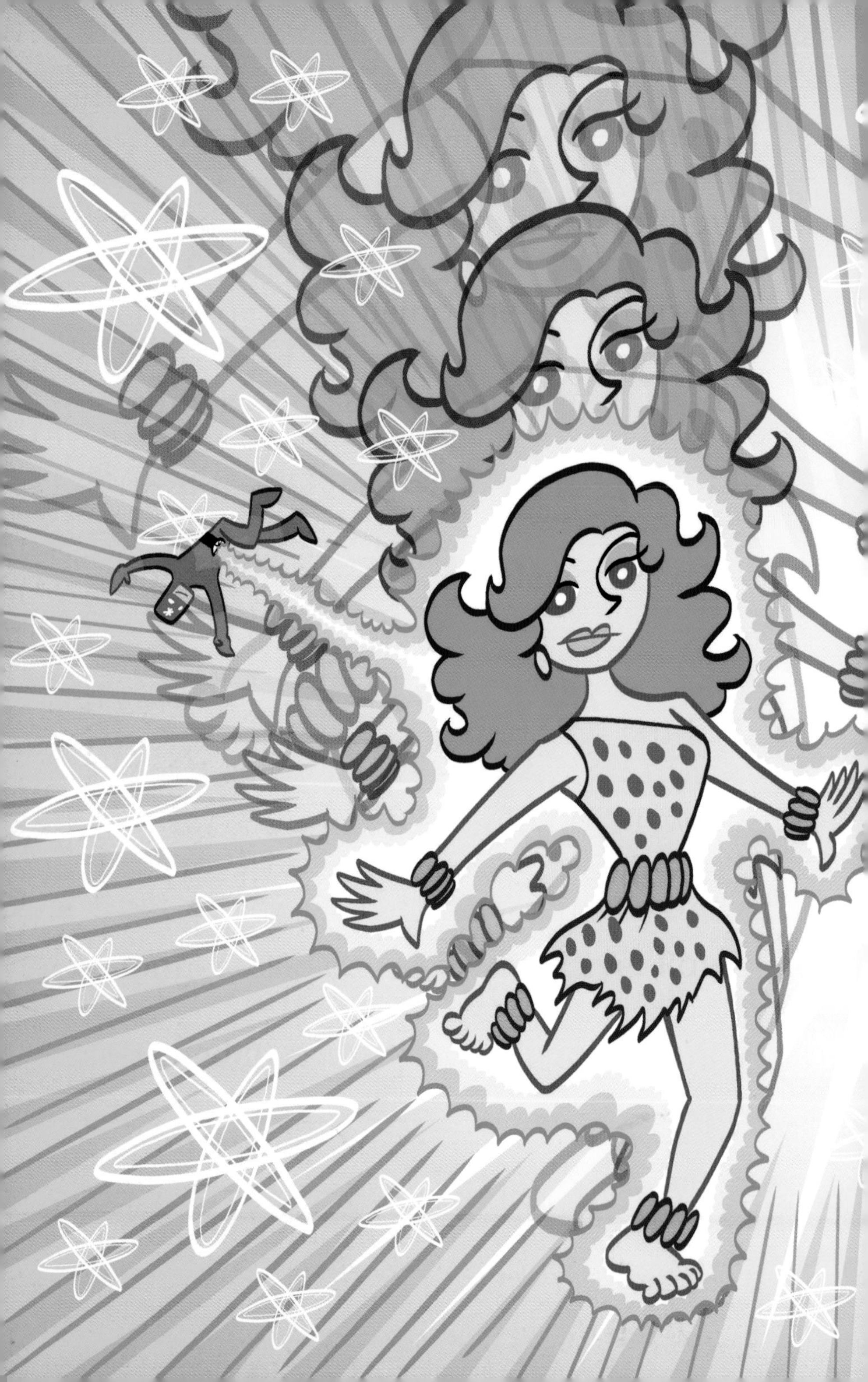

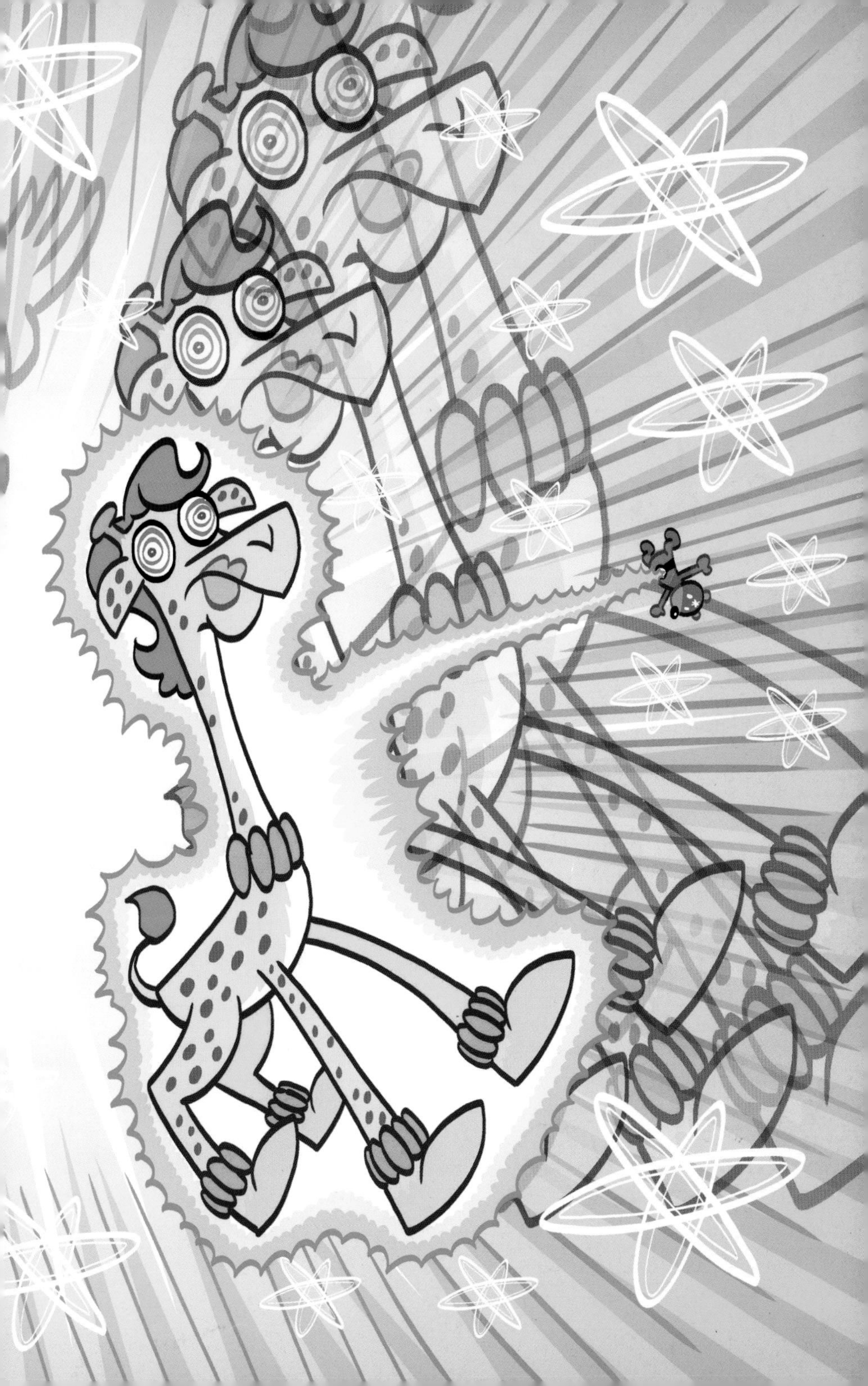

The terrible twosome fell onto the grass. They shrank back to their original sizes.

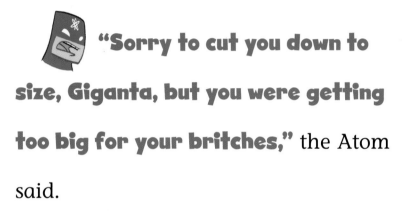 **"Sorry to cut you down to size, Giganta, but you were getting too big for your britches,"** the Atom said.

Dr. Zeul looked around at the park.

"What a mess I've made!" she cried. Patches nuzzled against Doris. **"But at least I made a new friend."**

Doris patted Patches as the police and animal rescue arrived.

The Atom and Spot stood by as the criminals were finally captured. Apache Chief was saddened by the situation. He believed everyone should get a second chance.

 "There must be some other way," he said to the police officers. "Please allow me to help."

"Thank you for your kindness," Dr. Zeul said, "but I can't show my face in public anymore. I have made a fool of myself and the science community."

"Perhaps science isn't your true calling," Apache Chief replied. "With the proper training, you and Patches can use your powers for good. I can make you star attractions at the Super Hero Show!"

Dr. Zeul was overwhelmed with joy. She slipped her handcuffs over the Chief and gave him a big hug.

*   *   *

Months later, the Super Hero Show returned to Ivy Town. Dr. Palmer and Spot had tickets to opening night. They came to see the newest performer, **Giganta the Strongwoman.**

When the curtains parted, Giganta emerged with Apache Chief and Patches.

Together, the new friends said the magic words: "Inuk-chuk!"

They each grew to fifty feet tall. Their performance was amazing. The crowd threw flowers and gave them a standing ovation.

"You see that, Spot?" Dr. Palmer said. "A small act of kindness can make a big difference."

 "Bark, bark, bark!" Spot agreed.

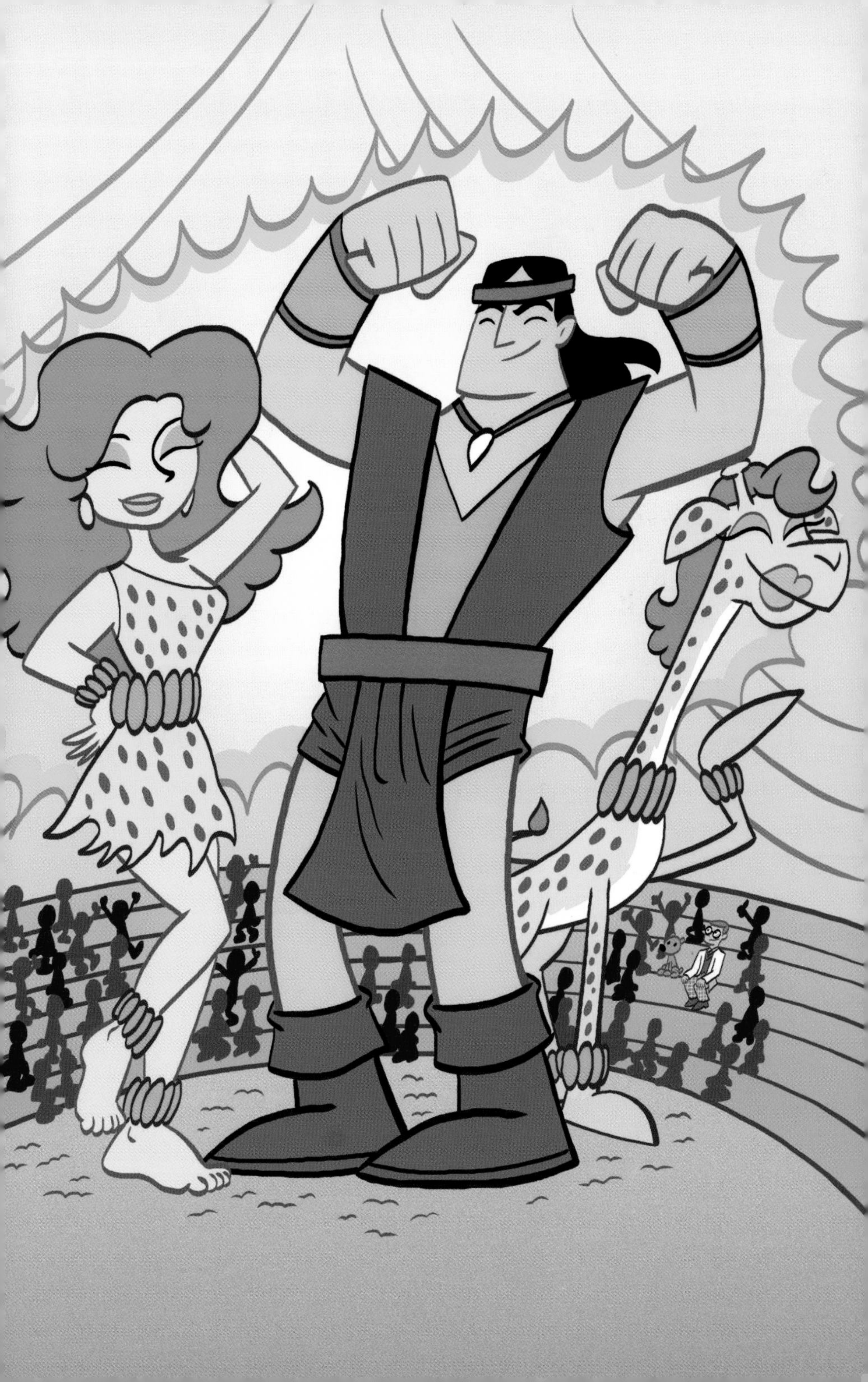

1. Krypto
2. Streaky
3. Whizzy
4. Comet
5. Beppo
6. Super-Turtle
7. Fuzzy
8. Ace
9. Robin Robin
10. Batcow
11. Jumpa
12. Whatzit
13. Hoppy
14. Tawky Tawny
15. Spot
16. Plastic Frog
17. Gleek
18. Big Ted
19. Dawg
20. Space Dolphins
21. Proty
22. Chameleon Collie
23. Bull Dog
24. Paw Pooch
25. Tusky Husky
26. Hot Dog
27. Tail Terrier
28. Mammoth Mutt
29. Prophetic Pup
30. Rex the Wonder Dog
31. Detective Chimp
32. Starlene
33. Mossy
34. Merle
35. Loafers
36. Storm
37. Topo
38. Ark
39. Fluffy
40. Betty
41. Geoffrey
42. B'dg
43. Sen-Tag
44. Fendor
45. Stripezoid
46. Zallion
47. Ribitz
48. Bzzd
49. Gratch
50. Buzzoo
51. Fossfur
52. Zhoomp
53. Eeny

KNOW YOUR HERO PETS!

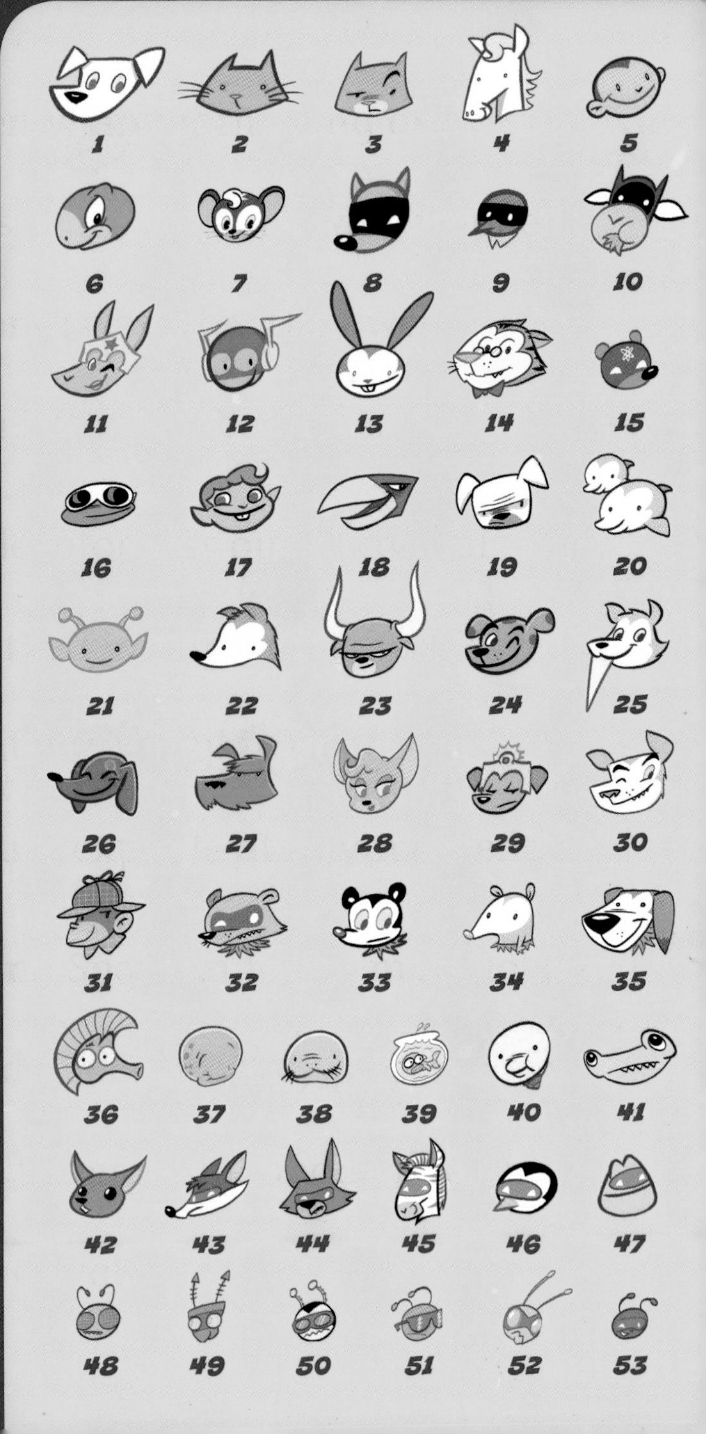

1
2
3
4
5
6
7
8
9
10
11
12
13
14
15
16
17
18
19
20
21
22
23
24
25
26
27
28
29
30
31
32
33
34
35
36
37
38
39
40
41
42
43
44
45
46
47
48
49
50
51
52
53

KNOW YOUR VILLAIN PETS!

1. Bizarro Krypto
2. Ignatius
3. Brainicat
4. Mechanikat
5. Dogwood
6. General Manx
7. Nizz
8. Fer-El
9. Crackers
10. Giggles
11. Artie Puffin
12. Griff
13. Waddles
14. Rozz
15. Mad Catter
16. Croward
17. Chauncey
18. Bit-Bit & X-43
19. Dr. Spider
20. Anna Conda
21. Mr. Mind
22. Sobek
23. Patches
24. Dex-Starr
25. Glomulus
26. Titano
27. Purring Pete
28. Kid Kitty
29. Scratchy Tom
30. Gat-Cat
31. Starro
32. Mama Ripples
33. Faye Precious
34. Limpy
35. Offie Lee
36. Misty
37. Sneezers
38. Johnny
39. Joey
40. Frankie
41. George
42. Whoosh
43. Pronto
44. Snorrt
45. Rolf
46. Squealer
47. Kajunn
48. Tootz
49. Eezix
50. Donald
51. Waxxee
52. Fimble
53. Webbik

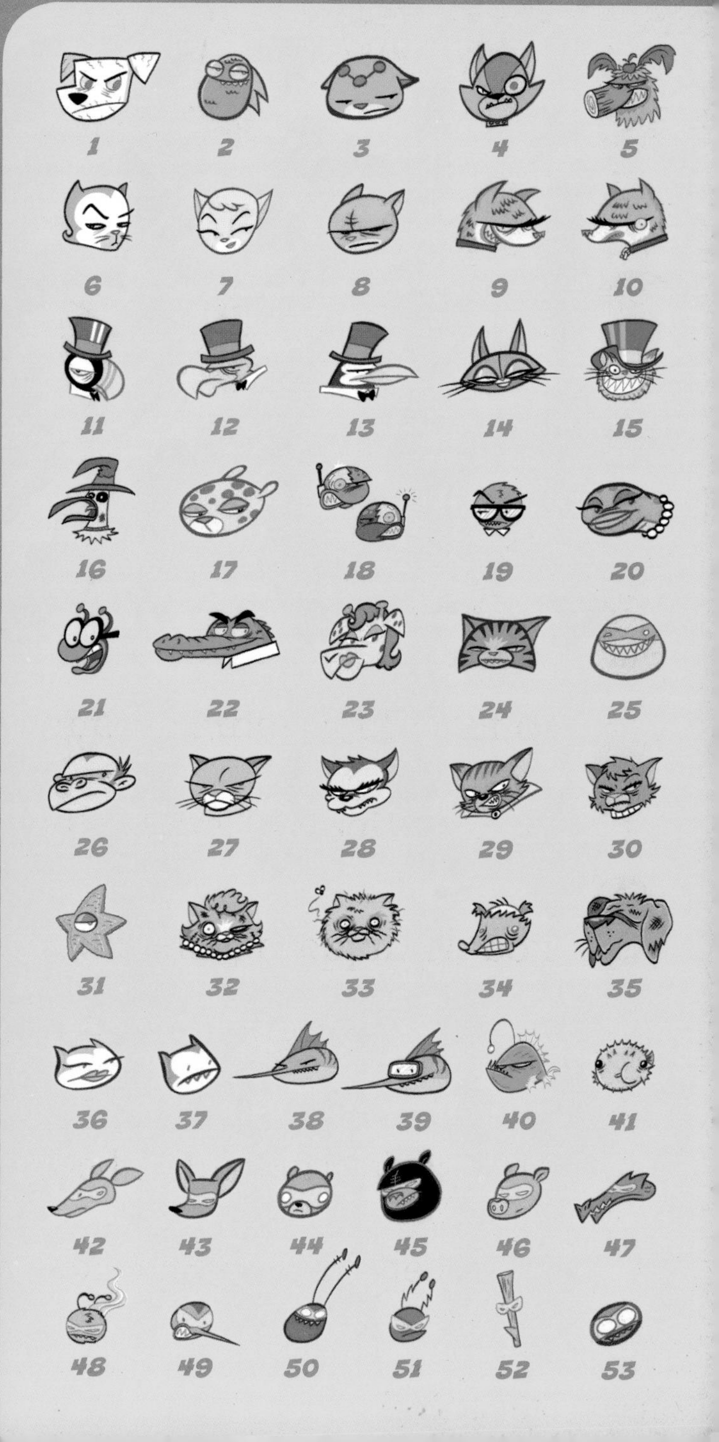

1 2 3 4 5
6 7 8 9 10
11 12 13 14 15
16 17 18 19 20
21 22 23 24 25
26 27 28 29 30
31 32 33 34 35
36 37 38 39 40 41
42 43 44 45 46 47
48 49 50 51 52 53

MEET THE AUTHOR!

John Sazaklis

John Sazaklis, a *New York Times* bestselling author, enjoys writing children's books about his favorite characters. To him, it's a dream come true. He has been reading comics and watching cartoons since before even the Internet! John lives with his beautiful wife in the Big Apple.

MEET THE ILLUSTRATOR!

Eisner Award-winner Art Baltazar

Art Baltazar is a cartoonist machine from the heart of Chicago! He defines cartoons and comics not only as an art style, but as a way of life. Currently, Art is the creative force behind *The New York Times* best-selling, Eisner Award-winning, DC Comics series Tiny Titans, and the co-writer for *Billy Batson and the Magic of SHAZAM!* Art is living the dream! He draws comics and never has to leave the house. He lives with his lovely wife, Rose, big boy Sonny, little boy Gordon, and little girl Audrey. Right on!

atom (AT-uhm)—the smallest part of an element that has all the properties of that element; everything is made up of atoms.

beaker (BEE-kur)—a plastic or glass jar with a spout for pouring, used in chemistry

dwarf star (DWORF STAR)—a star, such as the Sun, having low mass, small size, and average brightness

electron (i-LEK-tron)—a tiny particle that moves around the center of an atom and carries a negative charge

lens (LENZ)— a piece of curved glass used to magnify an object or focus light

magnifying glass (MAG-nuh-fye-ing GLASS)—a glass lens that makes things look bigger

university (yoo-nuh-VUR-suh-tee)—a school for higher learning after high school where people can study for degrees

HERO DOGS
GALORE!

SPACE CANINE
PATROL AGENCY!

KRYPTO THE
SUPER-DOG!

BATCOW!

FLUFFY AND THE
AQUA-PETS!

PLASTIC
FROG!

JUMPA
THE KANGA!

STORM AND THE
AQUA-PETS!

STREAKY
THE SUPER-CAT!

THE TERRIFIC
WHATZIT!

SUPER-TURTLE!

BIG TED
AND DAWG!

Read all of these totally awesome stories today, starring all of your favorite DC SUPER-PETS!

GREEN LANTERN BUG CORPS!

SPOT!

ROBIN ROBIN AND ACE TEAM-UP!

SPACE CANINE PATROL AGENCY!

HOPPY!

BEPPO THE SUPER-MONKEY!

ACE THE BAT-HOUND!

KRYPTO AND ACE TEAM-UP!

B'DG, THE GREEN LANTERN!

THE LEGION OF SUPER-PETS!

COMET THE SUPER-HORSE!

DOWN HOME CRITTER GANG!

Picture Window Books™

Published in 2013
A Capstone Imprint
1710 Roe Crest Drive
North Mankato, MN 56003
www.capstonepub.com

STAR26100

Cataloging-in-Publication Data is available at
the Library of Congress website.
ISBN: 978-1-4048-6490-0 (library binding)
ISBN: 978-1-4048-7664-4 (paperback)

Summary: When Dr. Ray Palmer and his
brainy bowwow, Spot, invent a shrinking
machine, rival scientist Doris Zuel gets jealous
— BIG TIME! She transforms into Giganta, the
world's tallest terror! In a battle of small versus
tall, the mighty mites must defeat this baddie
and her jumbo giraffe, Patches.

Art Director & Designer: Bob Lentz
Editor: Donald Lemke
Creative Director: Heather Kindseth
Editorial Director: Michael Dahl

Printed in the United States of America in
North Mankato, Minnesota.
122017   010972R

DC SUPER-PETS!™

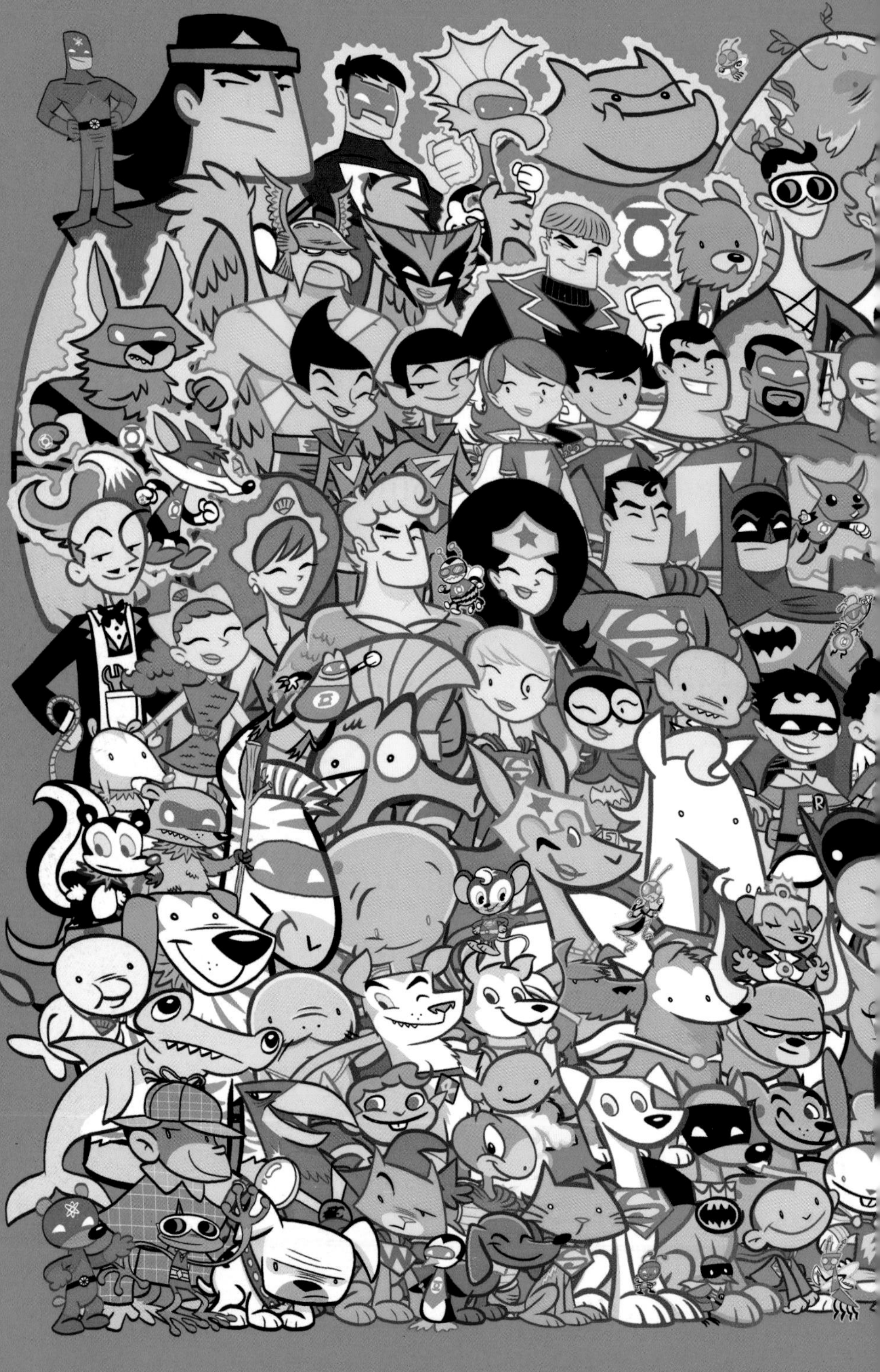